THE STEADFAST
TIN SOLDIER

By Hans Christian Andersen

Retold by Katie Cotton
Illustrated by Sophie Allsopp

templar publishing

IT WAS A LITTLE BOY'S BIRTHDAY, and he was busy unwrapping his gifts. "Tin soldiers!" he cried happily, as he opened the biggest box.

And what a sight they were! Twenty-five of them stood to attention in rows, straight and strong in their handsome red and blue uniforms.

They were all brothers, as they had been fashioned from the same tin spoon. Only one was a little different. He only had one leg, as he was the last to be cast and there wasn't quite enough tin. But he stood as straight and tall on his one leg as the others did on their two. As you shall see, this tin soldier was the most steadfast of them all.

From the table in the playroom this last tin soldier could see a magnificent castle, with pale blue turrets that stretched almost to the ceiling. Outside the castle was a little lake where swans liked to swim, admiring their reflections in the gleaming water. But this was not what had drawn the tin soldier's eye.

For in the entrance to this castle stood a ballerina, balanced with one leg tucked up beneath her and her arms stretched out as if she were about to embrace someone. She wore a white muslin dress with a blue ribbon, fastened with a metal spangle that glittered in the light from the window. She was very beautiful, but there was something sad and quiet in her gaze.

"How lovely she is," thought the tin soldier, "and she only has one leg, just like me. But I am a common soldier and she is beautiful, with a castle. She would never look at me."

Later, when all the children had gone to bed and the creatures of the night started to creep outside, the toys began to play. The nutcracker turned somersaults, the dolls had a tea-party and the train flew around his tracks, toot-tooting as he went. All was clatter and clamour, except for the tin soldier and the ballerina, who looked only at each other. Eventually, the tin soldier could bear it no longer.

"Beautiful ballerina," he said, "tell me – why are you so sad?"

The ballerina's sigh was like a whisper. "I am lonely," she said, "for I am never played with, just left to stand here by the castle."

The tin soldier said nothing, but shuffled towards her, so that he could take

her hand in his. The ballerina smiled shyly, and the two began to talk together.

Suddenly the clock struck twelve. A jack-in-the-box sprang up at once.

"Why are you talking to MY ballerina?" he screamed, leering over the

soldier with his black eyes and painted grin. With one swipe of his

huge head, he knocked the tin soldier off the

table, then disappeared

back into his box.

The next morning, as part of a little game, the boy put the one-legged soldier and the jack-in-the-box on the window sill. The minute the boy's back was turned, the jack sprang up and, with another swipe of his huge head, knocked the tin soldier out of the open window.

"Ha ha ha! That'll teach you to talk to MY ballerina!" he hissed.

Down, down, down the tin soldier tumbled to the street, where his bayonet stuck between two cobblestones. The boy noticed he was gone and came to search with his maid, but they didn't see him. The tin soldier lay on the grey pavement, lost and alone.

It began to rain; first one drop fell and then another and soon it was pouring. The tin soldier began to feel very cold and unhappy. "I wonder why the jack was so angry," he thought to himself. "I wouldn't mind if he spoke to the ballerina, though I love her so."

When the rain had stopped, two boys came by. "Look," said one of them, "there is a tin soldier. Let's make him into a sailor."

The boys made a little boat out of newspaper, put the tin soldier on board and let it sail away in the gutter. Away it went, fast as the wind, for it had rained so hard that the gutter was a raging torrent. The boys clapped as the boat rocked and roiled in the waves. The tin soldier trembled and quaked inside himself but he looked as steadfast as ever, standing straight and strong in his red and blue uniform.

The boat was swept down a drain and entered a gloomy tunnel nearly as dark as it had been inside the box. "If only the ballerina were here," thought the soldier, "then I wouldn't care if it were twice as dark as this."

Then in the flickering half-light there appeared a giant rat, with sharp yellow teeth and a grubby scarf tied around its thick neck. "Where is your money?" it snarled. "Give me your money! No one can use this tunnel without paying!"

The tin soldier was afraid, but he pretended not to hear him, and held more firmly onto his rifle. The current grew stronger, and the boat gathered speed. The rat ran after the boat, shouting "Stop him! Stop him!" Gnashing its teeth furiously, the rat lunged towards the tin soldier with its grimy claws.

The boat twisted out of the rat's hungry grasp and away, as the current grew faster and faster. The soldier could see light up ahead and relief flooded his tin heart. He was coming to the end of the tunnel.

But there was a deafening, roaring sound, and the tin soldier realised that the noise came from a huge waterfall before him. "This is the end," he thought. It was enough to make the boldest man afraid, but the tin soldier was as steadfast as ever. "I only wish that I could have seen the ballerina one last time," he sighed.

The brave little boat flew out of the tunnel and down the waterfall, spinning round and round as the angry waves dragged it under with terrible force. The tin soldier would have sunk down into the mud at the bottom of the river, had not a greedy fish swum by at just that moment and swallowed him up with a gulp.

It was darkest of all in the fish's belly, but the tin soldier lay there as steadfast as he had always been. The fish darted and dashed in the wildest manner; then suddenly it was still.

A little while later, a ray of light appeared and someone said, "Why, look at what I've found!" The fish had been caught, taken to the market, and bought for dinner. The soldier felt himself picked up around the waist by a kitchen maid, and saw that he was being carried through a busy, bustling kitchen. "Come, brave tin soldier," said the kitchen maid, cleaning him with her cloth, "I will tell the family of your adventure."

The tin soldier couldn't believe his eyes. He had been taken to the same playroom that he had left that morning! There was the little boy, and the nutcracker, and the train, and there - how his tin heart sang to see her - was his ballerina, still standing on one leg outside her castle. He looked at her, and she looked at him. She smiled shyly, for her heart was as steadfast as his.

The tin soldier was so touched he would have cried tin tears if he could have. Not one word was said, but the ballerina and the soldier continued to stare steadily, waiting for night to fall so they could be together once more.

But the evil jack-in-the-box had seen everything. Wild with jealousy, he nudged the tin soldier into the sight of a nasty little boy who was visiting, feared by all the toys because he treated them so badly. The boy took one look at the soldier, picked him up by his only leg, and carelessly threw him onto the fire.

The flames roared and crackled so fiercely that no one heard the tiny cry from the ballerina, as her heart broke. But everyone remarked that it was very strange, the way she seemed to fly across the room – almost as if she were a fairy – into the fire and the open arms of the tin soldier.

The next day, the maid was cleaning out the grate when she found a little tin heart and a metal spangle among the ashes. She wasn't sure whether to give them to the little boy, who had been so upset at his toys being burned. But she was glad she did, for he dried his eyes and smiled, softly.

"I mustn't be sad that I can't play with them any more," the little boy thought to himself as he buried the spangle and the heart in the garden. "They have each other, and they can play together."